The Adventures of Sam Pig

Sam Pig and the Wind

Alison Uttley

Illustrated by Graham Percy

faber and faber

LONDON · BOSTON

First published in 1940
by Faber and Faber Limited
3 Queen Square London WC1N 3AU
This edition first published in 1989

Printed in Great Britain by
W.S. Cowell Ltd Ipswich

British Library Cataloguing in Publication Data is available

ISBN 0–571–15295–3

Sam Pig and the Wind

It was washing day and Ann Pig decided that it was time Sam's trousers were put in the washtub. They were new trousers, you will remember, made of sheep's wool, dyed red and blue in large checks, but they were dirty, for Sam had fallen into a pool of mud and stuck there till he was rescued.

So Ann scrubbed and rubbed them and hung them up to dry on the clothes-line in the crab-apple orchard, where they fluttered among pyjamas and handkerchiefs and the rest of the family wash.

Sam Pig stood near, watching them, for he was afraid the Fox might steal them if he got the chance. It was a warm day, and Sam enjoyed having his little legs free.

'I'll stand on guard,' said he, 'then nobody can take my trousers for their nests or anything.'

The pair of trousers bobbed and danced on the clothes-line as if somebody were shaking them. It was the wind, which was blowing strongly. It came out of the clouds with a sudden swoop, and it puffed them and it huffed them, and it stuffed them with air. They really seemed to have a pair of invisible fat legs inside them as they swung to and fro and jigged and turned somersaults over the line.

The wind must have taken a fancy to those trousers for it gave a great tug and the wooden clothes-pegs fell to the ground. Sam Pig stooped to pick up his trousers, but they leapt away out of his grasp, and across the orchard. Sam sprang after them in a hurry. They frisked over the wall, struggled among the rough stones, and disappeared. Sam was sure they would be lying on the other side, and he climbed slowly and carefully to the top. Alas! The little trousers were already

running swiftly across the meadow, trundling along the ground as if a pair of stout legs were inside them. Sam jumped down and ran after them at full speed. He nearly reached them, for the wind dropped and the little trousers flapped and fell empty to the ground. Just as Sam's arm was outstretched to grab them the wind swept down with a howl and caught them up again. It whirled them higher and higher, and tossed them into a tree.

'Whoo-oo-oo,' whistled the wind, as it shook them and left them. There they dangled, caught in a branch, like a dejected ninny. Sam Pig was not daunted. He began to climb that tree. He was part way up, clasping the slippery trunk, panting as he looked for a foothold, when the trousers disentangled themselves and fell to the earth.

'Hurrah!' cried Sam, and he slithered down to safety. 'Hurrah! Now I can get them.'

No! The wind swept down upon them. They rose on their little balloon legs and danced away. The wind blew stronger, and the trousers took leaps in the air like an acrobat. They turned head over heels; they danced on one leg and then on the other, like a sailor doing the hornpipe. Never were such dancing trousers seen as those windy wind-bags!

'Give me back my trousers, O wind,' called Sam Pig, and the wind laughed 'Who-o-o-o. Who-o-o,' and shrieked, 'Noo-oo-oo,' in such a shrill high voice that Sam shivered with the icy coldness of it.

The trousers jigged along the meadows and into the woods, with Sam running breathlessly after them. He tripped over brambles and caught his feet in rabbit holes and tumbled over tree trunks, but the trousers, wide-legged and active, leapt over the briars, and escaped the thorns as

the wind tugged them away. When the wind paused a moment to take a deep breath Sam Pig got near, but he was never in time to catch the runaways. Sometimes they lay down for a rest, but as Sam crept up, stepping softly lest the wind should hear, they sprang to their invisible feet and scampered away.

'What's the matter, Sam?' asked the grey donkey when Sam ran past with his arms outstretched and his ears laid flat. 'Why are you running so fast?'

'My trousers! My trousers!' panted Sam. 'The wind's got them, and it's blowing them away.'

'My goodness! It will blow them across the world, Sam. You'll never see them again,' cried the donkey staring after the dancing garment. He kicked up his heels and brayed loudly and then galloped after them with his teeth bared.

'Hee-haw! Hee-haw! Stop! Stop!' he blared in his trumpet voice. But he couldn't catch them either, so he returned to his thistles, hee-hawing at the plight of poor Sam Pig.

The trousers were now running across a cornfield, and as they leapt over the stubble Sam was sure there was somebody inside them. It was an airy fellow, whose long transparent arms and

sea-green fingers waved and pointed to sky and earth. A laughing mocking face with puffed-out cheeks nodded at Sam, and a pursed-up mouth whistled shrilly. Wild locks of hair streamed from the wind's head. The thin eldritch voice shrieked like pipes playing, wailing and crying, now high, now low.

'Catch me! Catch me! Get me if you can! I'm the wind, Sam Pig. The wind! I'm the wind from the World's End. From the caves by the mad ocean, from the mountains snow-topped I come. I've flown a thousand leagues to play with you, Sam Pig! Catch me!'

'Wait a minute,' said Sam, rather crossly, and he trundled along on his fat little legs.

The wind turned round and danced about Sam, pulling his tail and blowing in his face so that the little pig had to shut his eyes. Suddenly the wind blew a hurricane. It picked him up and carried him in the air. How frightened was our little Sam Pig when he felt his feet paddling on nothing! His curly tail stuck out straight, his ears were flattened, his body cold as ice. He tried to call for help but no words came. Breathlessly he flew with his legs outstretched, his little feet pad-padding on the soft cushion of air.

Then the wind took pity on him, and dropped him lightly to the ground. He gave a pitiful squeak and lay panting and puffing with fright. He opened his eyes and saw his trousers lying near. He edged towards them and put out a hand, but the trousers stood up, shook themselves full of air, and went dancing off. ·

Sam Pig arose and followed after. He was a strong-hearted little pig and he was determined not to lose his beloved trousers.

The wind carried them to the farmyard, and sent them fluttering their flapping sides among the hens. The cock crowed, the hens all ran helter-skelter, and the trousers trotted here and there among them, ruffling their feathers, blowing them about like leaves. Sam Pig scrambled over the gate and ran to them, trying to catch the elusive trousers, but getting the cock's tail instead.

'Stop it! Catch it! Catch the wind!' cried Sam.

'Nobody can catch the wind,' crowed the cock. 'Cockadoodle doo! Take shelter, my little red wives!' And the little hens crouched together in a bunch.

'Puff! Puff! Whoo-oo-oo!' screamed the wind,

blowing out its cheeks, and prancing in the little checked trousers belonging to Sam Pig.

'Quick! Catch it!' called Sam lustily, and he puffed and blew and scampered on aching little legs trying to get the wind, as it whirled round the farmyard.

The wind blew in a sudden gust and the trousers flew over the gate into the field where the cattle grazed.

'Boo-hoo-oo-oo-oo,' it howled, and it raced round the field blowing the cows so that they fled to the walls and stood within the shelter. But the pair of trousers with the wind inside leapt on to

the back of a young heifer and sat astride,
puffing into her hairy ears, holding her horns
with long thin fingers.

She leapt forward in a fright and the wind
rode on her back-bone, standing on one leg, like
a circus rider. After her went Sam Pig calling,
'Stop! Catch the wind! Give me my trousers!'

'You can't catch the wind, Sam Pig,' mooed the
cows from their shelter. 'You can hide till it's past
but you can't catch it.'

Down from the cow's back leapt the trousers,
and away they jigged and pranced over the grass,
twirling at a great pace, with Sam Pig's little legs

plodding faithfully after. He was running so fast his legs seemed to twinkle, but the wind went faster, and the trousers now rose in the air like a kite and now paddled over the ground, luring Sam on by pretending to droop and die.

In the next field was Sally the mare. With a whoop and a cry the wind seized her mane and dragged at her long tail. She turned her back and even when the little trousers leapt on to her haunches, she took no notice.

'Get on! Gee-up! Whoo oo oo to you,' cried the wind, angrily kicking her ribs with invisible toes, and thumping her sides with the empty legs of

the checked trousers. The mare stood stock still, head bent, eyes closed, refusing to budge an inch. Sam Pig came hurrying up to his old friend.

'Oh Sally! Catch the wind! Keep the wind from taking my trousers away. Hold it, Sally!'

'You can't catch the wind, little Sam. It's free to blow where it likes, and nobody can tame it,' muttered Sally. 'But I won't move for any wind that blows.'

So the wind leapt away and skipped across the fields. The long grasses all turned with it, and tried to follow, but the earth held them back. The trees bent their boughs and the leaves tugged and broke from the twigs and flew after the swift-moving wind.

'There goes the wind,' cried the trees, and they stretched their green fingers in the way the wind had gone.

The wind blew next along a country lane, and the little trousers scampered between the flowery banks with Sam Pig following after. They reached the high road, and Sam hesitated a moment, for he never went alone on the King's Highway. But he was determined to catch his checked trousers. Clouds of white dust rose and

came after them, pieces of paper were caught
and whirled in the air, and a poor butterfly was
torn from its flower and swept up in the whirl-
pool of motion after the flying trousers with the
wind inside them.

An old woman walked along the road. Her
shawl was tightly wrapped round her shoulders,
her bonnet fastened with a ribbon, and her black
shoes latched on her feet. In her hand she
grasped a green umbrella of prodigious size. It
was the old witch-woman going to the village to
do her marketing.

'Drat the wind! It's raising a mighty dust! It will spoil my best bonnet,' she murmured to herself as she saw the cloud of white dust sweeping upon her. She opened the big umbrella and held it over her bonnet. But the wind shot out a long arm and grasped the green umbrella. It snatched it from her hand and bore it away inside out.

She gave a cry of dismay and bent her head to keep her bonnet from being torn from its ribbons. She clutched her shawl and shut her eyes which watered with the dust.

'My poor old umbereller! It's gone! It's seen many a storm of wind and rain, but never a gust as sharp as this!'

The wind passed on, and she ventured to raise her eyes. In the distance she could see the green

umbrella flying along, and a pair of trousers running under it, and after them a short fat pig.

'Poor crittur!' she cried. 'A little pig, and it looks like my own friend little Pigwiggin as came to see me once upon a time! He's blown away by this terrible varmint of a wind!'

The wind and Sam came to a church with a weathercock on top of the tower. The iron cock looked down in alarm. It spun round on its creaking axis, and crackled its stiff feathers. Backwards went the wind, and back went the weathercock, groaning with pain, and back went Sam Pig, and back went the trousers and the umbrella and all. Away they went over the fields, taking the shortest cut, over the brook and up the hill. Sam Pig saw that the wind was heading, or

legging, for home. His own little legs were tired
and bleeding, his feet were sore, and his eyes red
with dust and wind, but he kept on.

There was the little house at the edge of the
wood, and there the little stream with Ann filling
the kettle, and there the drying-ground with the
clothes-line, empty and forlorn between the crab-
apple trees.

The wind bustled over the grass and stopped
dead. The pair of trousers fell in a heap. The

green umbrella lay with its ribs sticking out. Its horn handle and thick cotton cover were unharmed for it had lived a hundred years already and weathered many a gale.

'Give me back my trousers,' said Sam, in a tired little voice.

'Take thy trousers,' answered the wind, and it shook the trousers and dropped them again.

Sam Pig leapt with a last great effort upon his trousers, and held them down. They never offered to move, for the wind had died away, and the air was still.

'Where are you, wind? Where have you gone?' asked Sam when he recovered himself sufficiently to speak. There was silence except for a faint whisper near the ground. Sam put his ear to a harebell's lip, and from it came the clear tiny tinkle of a baby wind which was curled up inside and going to sleep.

'Good-bye, Sam Pig,' said this very small whisper of a voice. 'Good-bye. I gave you a fine run, Sam Pig, and you were a good follower.'

'Good-bye, wind,' murmured Sam, and he sighed and lay down with his head on his trousers. He fell asleep in a twinkling.

There Ann found him when she came to the orchard to collect the clothes-pegs. On the ground lay Sam, with his face coated with dust, but smiling happily. His little feet were stained and cut, his arm outstretched over his torn trousers. By him was a green umbrella, inside out, a gigantic umbrella which would shelter all the family of pigs and Badger too, if they sat under it.

Ann carefully turned it the right way. Then she stooped and gave her brother a shake.

'Sam! Sam! Wake up!' she called. 'Sam! Where have you been?'

Sam rubbed his eyes and yawned. Then he sat up.

'Oh Sam! There was such a wind as you never saw! It blew the clothes off the line and I found them lying here, all except your trousers. Oh, poor Sam! I thought it had blown them right away, but here they are, under your head.'

'Yes, Ann,' said Sam, yawning again. 'The wind carried them off. I saw it with my own eyes. It ran a long, long way, but I ran too, and I caught it and got my trousers back again.'

'You caught the wind? You got your trousers back from the raging, roaring wind?' asked Ann in astonishment.

'Yes,' Sam nodded proudly, and he opened his mouth, and shut it again. 'I ran about a hundred miles. I raced the wind, and I wouldn't let it keep my trousers.'

'And what's this?' asked Ann, holding up the green umbrella.

'Oh, that belongs to the nice old witch-woman. I passed her on the way, and the wind snatched it from her. I'll take it back sometime. I'm so sleepy, Ann. Do leave me alone.'

Sam's head dropped on the trousers, and he fell fast asleep. So Badger carried him in and put him to bed. Ann mended the adventurous trousers which the wind had torn. She turned out the pockets and found a small ancient whistle, which somebody had left there.

'Don't touch it,' warned Badger. 'Don't blow it. It's the wind's own whistle. Don't you know the saying, "Whistle for the wind"? If ever Sam wants the wind to come he has only to blow the whistle. We don't want it now, but if ever we do it will come.'

He put the whistle in a safe place on a top shelf, and there it lay for many a day, forgotten by everybody.

'It's an ill wind that blows nobody good,' observed Bill wisely. 'That long run has made young Sam as slim as a sapling. It is remarkable what a difference the wind makes to a fat little pig's figure.'

'But it was a good run,' said Tom. 'To think that our little Sam caught the wind.'

'Nobody else could do that,' said Ann. They were all very proud of little Sam Pig.